THE SHADOW IN THE MOON

A Tale of the Mid-Autumn Festival

CHRISTINA MATULA

ILLUSTRATED BY PEARL LAW

Charlesbridge

For Elsa & Sandor—C. M.

To my parents and to my grandfather, who
patiently took me around the markets for hours
to search for my perfect lantern—P. L.

Text copyright © 2018 by Christina Matula
Illustrations copyright © 2018 by Pearl Law

Published by Charlesbridge
85 Main Street
Watertown, MA 02472
(617) 926-0329
www.charlesbridge.com

Library of Congress Cataloging-in-Publication Data
Names: Matula, Christina, author. | Law, Pearl, illustrator.
Title: The shadow in the Moon: a tale of the Mid-Autumn Festival/Christina Matula;
    illustrated by Pearl Law.
Description: Watertown, MA: Charlesbridge, [2018] | Summary: Two young sisters celebrate the
    Mid-Autumn Festival, admire their mooncakes decorated with a picture of a lady in the moon,
    and listen to their Ah-ma tell the ancient tale of how the holiday began.
Identifiers: LCCN 2017003931 (print) | LCCN 2017022714 (ebook) | ISBN 9781632895639 (ebook) |
    ISBN 9781632895646 (ebook pdf) | ISBN 9781580897464 (reinforced for library use)
Subjects: LCSH: Mid-autumn Festival—Juvenile fiction. | Harvest festivals—China—Juvenile fiction. |
    Folklore—China—Juvenile fiction.| Moon—Folklore—Juvenile fiction. | CYAC: Mid-autumn
    Festival—Folklore. | Moon—Folklore. | Folklore—China.
Classification: LCC PZ8.1.M438 (ebook) | LCC PZ8.1.M438 Sh 2018 (print) | DDC 398.2 [E]—dc23
LC record available at https://lccn.loc.gov/2017003931

Printed in China
(hc) 10 9 8 7 6 5 4 3 2 1

For this book, I penciled all the drawings first, scanned them, then I used Photoshop to paint over
    them. At the time I was working on this, I was obsessed with the "Dissolve" brush effect, which
    achieved the grainy look in most backgrounds.
Display type hand lettered by Pearl Law
Text type set in Helenita
Color separations by Colourscan Print Co Pte Ltd, Singapore
Printed by 1010 Printing International Limited in Huizhou, Guangdong, China
Production supervision by Brian G. Walker
Designed by Susan Mallory Sherman

Tonight is our Mid-Autumn Festival feast.
My sister and I watch as the whole family gathers in our home.

This is the time of year when the moon is biggest and brightest. It is when we celebrate and give thanks for the harvest. Our family comes together and becomes whole again, like the whole, full moon. First we look to the moon and give thanks, and then we make a wish for the coming year. This year, I'm still not sure what to wish for.

My favorite part of dinner is when we share mooncakes as small as my hand and as round as the moon. They have a flaky crust and a yummy filling. We cut the tiny cakes into wedges, and everyone takes a slice. My little sister likes the red bean ones. I like the lotus seed mooncakes best.

Our mooncakes are decorated with the form of a beautiful lady.

"Who is this lady?" I ask my grandmother.

"Chang'e, the Spirit and Lady in the Moon," Ah-ma replies.

"Please tell us about her!" my sister begs.
And so Ah-ma begins her story.

"There was a time long ago, in a place far away," Ah-ma says, "when ten suns kept the earth warm, taking turns shining one by one each day."

"But soon they became bored with this routine and decided to come out all at once. The earth quickly became too hot, and the people suffered. Although the heavens pleaded with them to stop, the suns were having too much fun to listen."

"Hou Yi, a young archer, watched the crops burn and the rivers dry up. He could no longer bear to see his people in distress. He headed east until he reached the suns. There, he asked them to shine one by one each day. When the suns refused, he shot down nine of them, leaving only one high in the sky. Hou Yi told this final sun to share the sky with the moon."

My sister and I listen eagerly. We want to know what happens next. "Hou Yi returned home to Chang'e, his loving wife. Chang'e was known to all as kind of heart and wise of mind. The people rejoiced, for life soon returned to normal. With only one sun in the sky, rivers flowed, crops grew, and the air was filled with happiness."

"News of Hou Yi's bravery spread throughout the land. It reached the Immortals, who lived in the heavens above the clouds. They gave Hou Yi a magic potion for his courage. It was a potion that would let him live forever as one of the Immortals in the sky."

"Hou Yi and Chang'e knew that this potion was very powerful. If it fell into the wrong hands, it would bring trouble. To keep it safe, they hid it in the cupboard."

Ah-ma pauses and lowers her voice. "But a thief was lurking outside the window and devised a plan to steal the potion for himself."

My sister and I hold our breath.

"Later, when Chang'e was home alone, the thief burst in and demanded the potion. She realized that giving the potion to someone as dangerous and greedy as a thief would bring grief to both the heavens and the earth. Before the thief could get to the cupboard, Chang'e grabbed the potion and swallowed it in one gulp."

"Suddenly, Chang'e felt her body become lighter. Her toes lifted off the floor. She floated through the window, into the sky, and up to the moon. There, as an Immortal, she would live forever. She became Chang'e, the Spirit and Lady in the Moon."

"Hou Yi returned home later that day. The cupboard door was open, the potion bottle was empty, and his wife was missing. He searched for her all day and into the night, but he could not find his beloved Chang'e.

"After countless hours, Hou Yi paused to rest and gaze up at the sky. He noticed that the moon seemed to have a new shadow. This shadow looked like a beautiful lady. Hou Yi suddenly remembered the magic potion and its promise of eternal life. He wondered if his beautiful wife could have taken the potion and floated to the sky.

"With a heavy heart, he realized that Chang'e was on earth no longer."

"Do not be sad, my loves," Ah-ma gently tells us. "From that day onward, Hou Yi would sit in his garden and gaze lovingly at the moon. Chang'e would reply by beaming her moonlight so bright. On the anniversary of the day his wife became the Spirit and Lady in the Moon, Hou Yi would put out her favorite foods, like round cakes and fresh fruit, to remind her that she was still in his heart.

"Those round cakes," Ah-ma says, "are what we now call mooncakes. And that, my girls, is the tale of two brave souls whose courage gave us peace and harmony between the heavens and the earth."

We breathe a sigh of relief and eat another slice of mooncake. When no one is looking, I slip a small piece into my pocket.

My belly is filled with food from our feast. My head is spinning with thoughts of suns, arrows, and magic potions. My heart is bursting with thanks for the bravery of Hou Yi and Chang'e.

I tell my family I am thankful for them, especially wise Ah-ma.
Maybe even for my little sister.

When the table is cleared, we gather our paper lanterns and head to the park to admire the full moon. As Chang'e beams brightly on us, I think about what I will wish this year.

I take the mooncake from my pocket and leave it by the side
of a tree, under the light of the moon. I close my eyes and send
my wish up to Chang'e, the Spirit and Lady in the Moon. I whisper,
"This year, I wish to be kind of heart and wise of mind."

Author's Note

Mid-Autumn Festival is one of the most important festivals in Chinese culture and is widely believed to be based on the folktale of Hou Yi and Chang'e. In the lunar calendar, Mid-Autumn falls on the fifteenth day of the eighth month, which is either in September or October. It is celebrated in China, Taiwan, Hong Kong, and Singapore, as well as neighboring countries like Japan, Korea, Malaysia, and Vietnam.

The festival always happens during a full moon, when the moon is at its biggest and brightest of the season. This is why it is also called the Moon Festival. The full moon is a symbol of reunion, as family members from far and wide travel home to reunite and celebrate. Those who are not able to be with their families can gaze at the moon and think of home and loved ones. "Quiet Night Thoughts," a poem by Li Bai, one of China's greatest poets, is said to be about missing his family when he couldn't be home to celebrate Mid-Autumn Festival. The poem is still studied today by schoolchildren throughout China. This is an English translation:

Before my bed there is bright moonlight
So that it seems like frost on the ground;
Lifting my head I watch the bright moon,
Lowering my head I dream that I'm home.

Mooncakes with Red-Bean Filling

As you make mooncakes with help from an adult, you will need a mold to give the mooncake its shape and design on the top. They come in all sorts of different designs. You can also use a silicone cookie mold, or you can shape them by hand to make little Jade Rabbits by decorating the dough balls with dough rabbit ears and poking holes for eyes. The Jade Rabbit is said to be Chang'e's companion on the moon.

Ingredients

4 tbsp golden syrup (light corn syrup)
water mixture: 1 tsp water with 1 tsp baking soda
¼ tsp vanilla extract
3 tbsp vegetable oil

1 cup all-purpose flour
1 small can (7 oz or 200g) sweetened red-bean paste
egg wash: 1 egg mixed with 1 tbsp water

- In a large bowl, mix the golden syrup, water mixture, vanilla, and oil, then add the flour. Mix gently. Knead the dough for a minute and set aside for 40 minutes.
- Preheat the oven to 350°F (175°C).
- On a floured surface, roll the dough into a cylinder (1 inch in diameter) and cut into 12 equal pieces.
- Roll each piece into a ball and flatten with your hand to make a small circle (2 to 3 inches wide), not too thin.
- Place a large rounded spoonful of the red-bean paste in the center of each dough circle, wrap it and pinch the seams, then gently roll it into a ball shape.
- Place each ball in the mooncake mold and press. Transfer the mooncakes to a baking sheet.
- Bake the mooncakes for 7 minutes, remove from the oven, and brush on the egg wash with a baking brush.
- Place the baking sheet back in the oven and bake the mooncakes for another 5 minutes, until golden brown. Let sit for 10 minutes, then remove from the baking sheet.
- Serve when cool (they taste even better the next day!).